Up, Up and Away

Written by Monica Hughes

Up go the bubbles,
up, up and away.

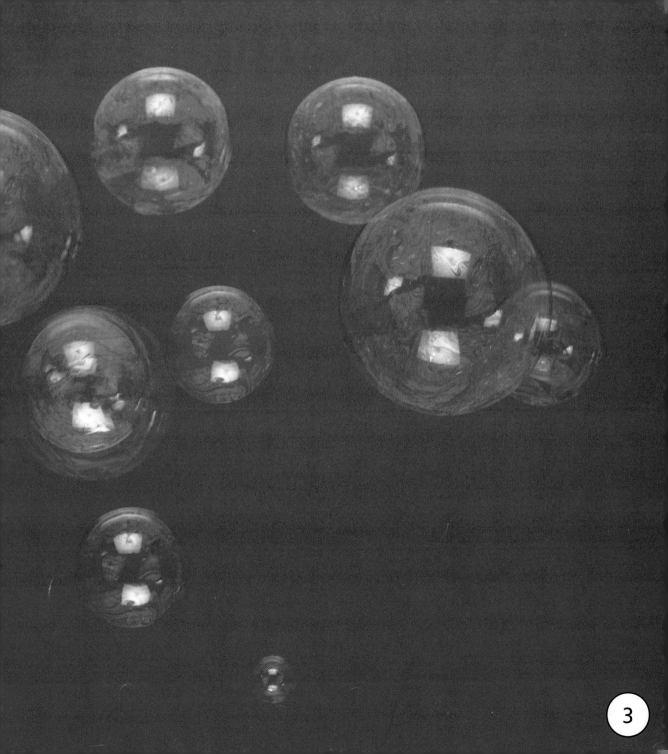

Up go the fireworks,
up, up and away.

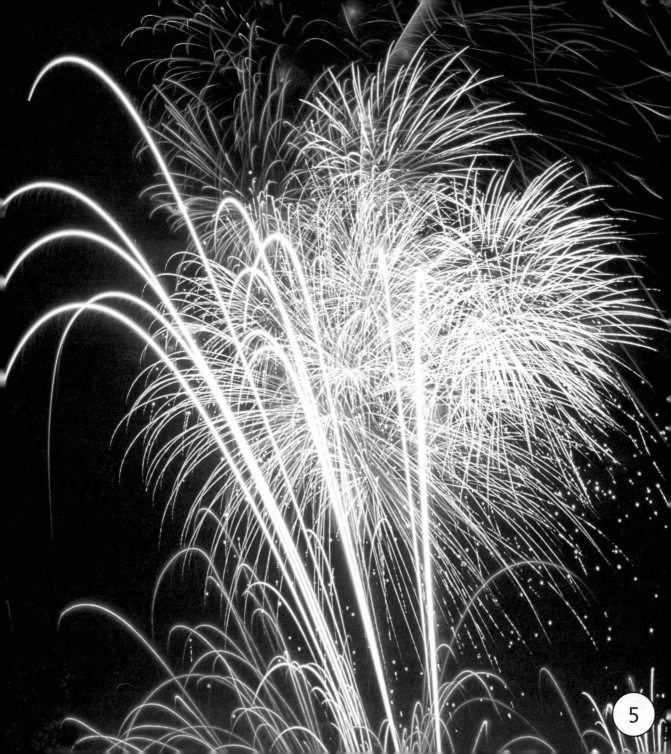

Up go the balloons,
up, up and away.

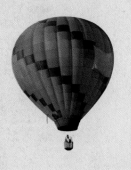
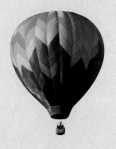
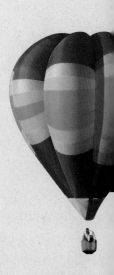

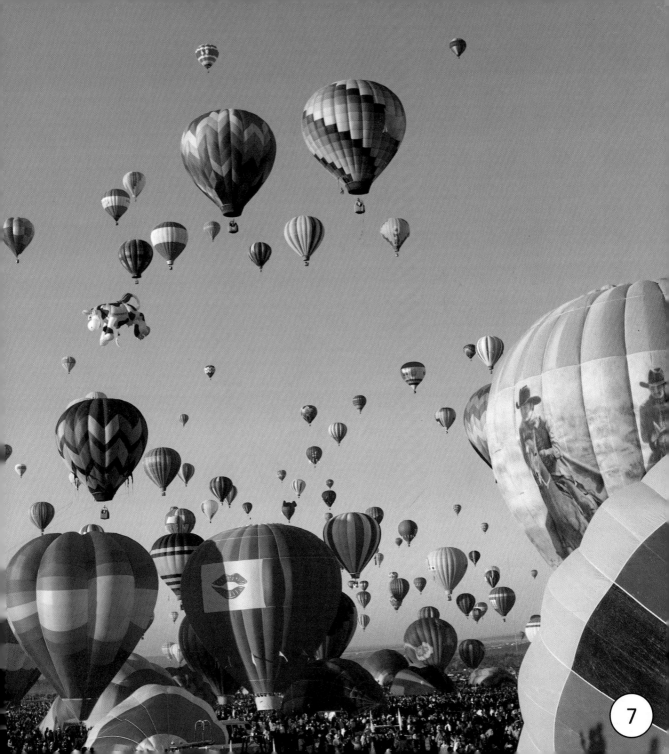

Up go the birds,
up, up and away.

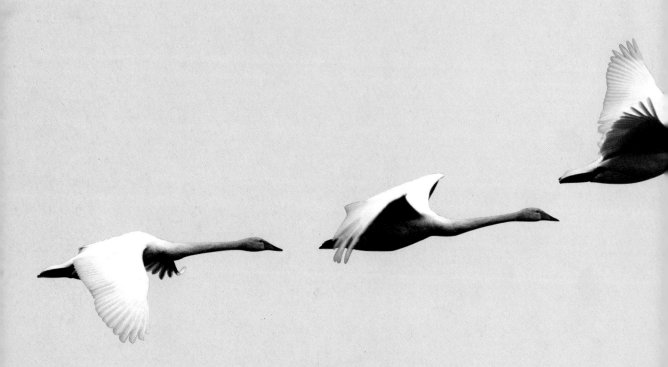

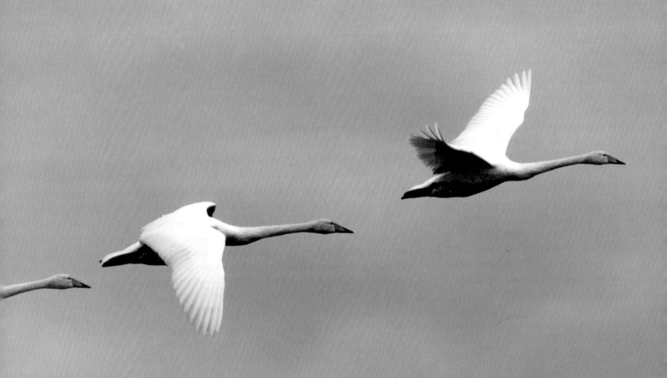

Up go the planes ...

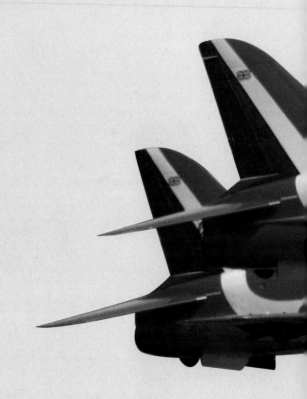

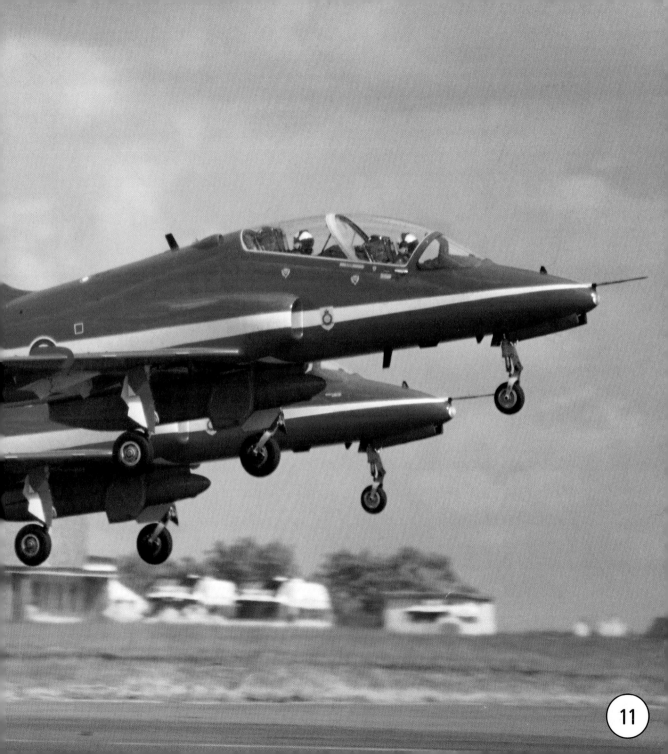

...up, up and away.